★ "This brief novel gets at the heart of a society that asks its citizens, even its children, to report on relatives and friends. Appropriately menacing illustrations by first-time novelist Yelchin add a sinister tone."
—*The Horn Book*, starred review

"Picture book author/illustrator Yelchin makes an impressive middle-grade debut with this compact novel about a devoted young Communist in Stalin-era Russia, illustrated with dramatically lit spot art." —*Publishers Weekly*

"Yelchin skillfully combines narrative with dramatic black-and-white illustrations to tell the story of life in the Soviet Union under Stalin. . . . An absorbing, quick, multilayered read." —*School Library Journal*

"Yelchin's graphite illustrations are an effective complement to his prose, which unfurls in Sasha's steady, first-person voice, and together they tell an important tale." —*Kirkus Reviews*

"This is serious, sophisticated stuff. The cat-and-mouse chase that pits Sasha's whole world against him will rivet middle-grade readers, but this title will hold special appeal for older students whose grasp of content outstrips their reading proficiency." —*The Bulletin of the Center for Children's Books*

"Yelchin's award winner will serve as a *1984* for the grade school set and will be an important conversation starter that teaches the nature of innocence in a time of great evil." —*The Jewish Journal*

"Transcends time and place . . . touching, beautiful and important."
—*Palo Alto Daily News*

BREAKING STALIN'S NOSE

BREAKING STALIN'S NOSE

WRITTEN AND ILLUSTRATED BY

EUGENE YELCHIN

SQUARE
FISH

HENRY HOLT AND COMPANY

NEW YORK

SQUARE FISH

An imprint of Macmillan Publishing Group, LLC
120 Broadway,
New York, NY 10271
mackids.com

Library of Congress Cataloging-in-Publication Data
Yelchin, Eugene.
Breaking Stalin's nose / Eugene Yelchin.
p.   cm.
Summary: In the Stalinist era of the Soviet Union, ten-year-old Sasha idolizes his
father, a devoted Communist, but when police take his father away and leave Sasha
homeless, he is forced to examine his own perceptions, values, and beliefs.
ISBN 978-1-250-03410-6 (paperback) / ISBN 978-1-4299-4995-8 (e-book)
1. Soviet Union—History—1925–1953—Juvenile fiction.
[1. Soviet Union—History—1925–1953—Fiction. 2. Communism—Fiction.
3. Fathers and sons—Fiction.] I. Title.
PZ7.Y3766Br 2011   [Fic]—dc22   2011005792

Originally published in the United States by Henry Holt and Company
First Square Fish Edition: 2013
Book designed by April Ward
Square Fish logo designed by Filomena Tuosto

15   17   19   20   18   16

AR: 2.0 / LEXILE: 670L

To my father,
who survived the Great Terror

MY DAD IS A HERO and a Communist and, more than anything, I want to be like him. I can never be like Comrade Stalin, of course. He's our great Leader and Teacher.

The voice on the radio says, "Soviet people, follow our great Leader and Teacher—the beloved Stalin—forward and ever forward to Communism! Stalin is our banner! Stalin is our future! Stalin is our happiness!" Then a song comes on, "A Bright Future Is Open to Us." I know every word, and, singing along, I take out a pencil and paper and start writing.

Dear Comrade Stalin,

I want to thank you personally for my happy childhood. I am fortunate to live in the Soviet Union, the most democratic and progressive country in the world. I have read how hard the lives of children are in the capitalist countries and I feel pity for all those who do not live in the USSR. They will never see their dreams come true.

My greatest dream has always been to join the Young Soviet Pioneers—the most important step in becoming a real Communist like my dad. By the time I was one year old, my dad had taught me the Pioneers greeting. He would say, "Young Pioneer! Ready to fight for the cause of the Communist Party and Comrade Stalin?" In response, I would raise my hand in the Pioneers salute.

CHAPTER 1

Of course, I couldn't reply "Always ready!" like the real Pioneers do; I couldn't talk yet. But I'm old enough now and my dream is becoming a reality. Tomorrow at my school's Pioneers rally, I will finally become a Pioneer.

It's not possible to be a true Pioneer without training one's character in the Stalinist spirit.

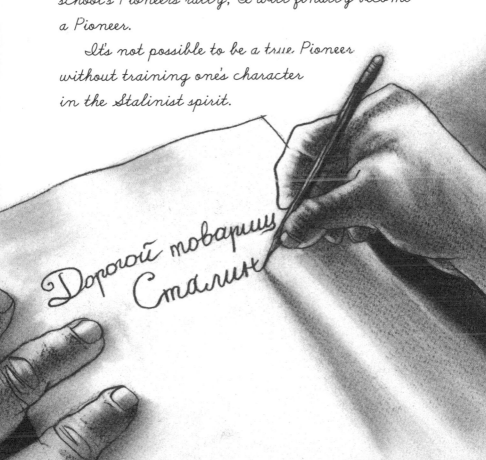

I solemnly promise to make myself strong from physical exercise, to forge my Communist character, and always to be vigilant, because our capitalist enemies are never asleep. I will not rest until I am truly useful to my beloved Soviet land and to you personally, dear Comrade Stalin. Thank you for giving me such a wonderful opportunity.

Forever yours,
Sasha Zaichik,
Moscow Elementary School #37

When I imagine Comrade Stalin reading my letter, I get so excited that I can't sit still. I rise up and march like a Pioneer around the room, then head to the kitchen to wait for my dad.

IT'S DINNERTIME, so the kitchen is crowded. Forty-eight hardworking, honest Soviet citizens share the kitchen and single small toilet in our communal apartment we call *komunalka* for short. We live here as one large, happy family: We are all equal; we have no secrets. We know who gets up at what time, who eats what for dinner, and who said what in their rooms. The walls are thin; some don't go up to the ceiling. We even have a room cleverly divided with shelves of books about Stalin that two families can share.

Stalin says that sharing our living space teaches us to think as Communist "WE" instead of capitalist "I." We agree. In the morning, we often sing patriotic songs together when we line up for the toilet.

OUR NEIGHBOR Marfa Ivanovna gives me a treat—
a carrot. I take the carrot to the kitchen window,
climb a warm radiator, and look down into the
courtyard to see if my dad is coming. Sometimes he
doesn't come home till morning. That is because he
works in the State Security on Lubyanka Square.

The State Security is our secret police, and their job is to unmask the disguised enemies infiltrating our borders. My dad is one of their best. Comrade Stalin personally pinned the order of the Red Banner on his chest and called him "an iron broom purging the vermin from our midst."

I take small bites of the carrot to make it last; the carrot is delicious. When hunger gnaws inside my belly, I tell myself that a future Pioneer has to repress cravings for such unimportant matters as food. Communism is just over the horizon; soon there will be plenty of food for everyone. But still, it's good to have something tasty to eat now and then. I wonder what it's like in the capitalist countries. I wouldn't be surprised if children there had never even tasted a carrot.

EVERYONE IN THE KITCHEN stops talking when my dad comes in. They look like they are afraid, but I know they are just respectful. Dad swoops me off the radiator and carries me through the kitchen, nodding at everybody. His overcoat is coarse and smells of snow. One neighbor, Stukachov, follows us down the corridor, smiling and bobbing his head, asking how many spies my dad has exposed today. Not that my dad would tell him—it's a state secret. But he catches enemies every day; that I know. He told me if I see a suspicious character on the street,

I should follow him and observe his activities; he might be a spy. It's wise to be suspicious. The enemies are everywhere.

When we get to our room, Stukachov is still trailing after us. I wish he would leave us alone and go to his own room, even though I know how crammed it is in there with his wife, three little kids, and mother. My dad and I have a large room for the two of us. I'm so embarrassed we live in luxury that I don't look at Stukachov, but I know he's there, stretching his neck and looking into our room when my dad closes the door on him.

"Don't talk to him," says my dad. "He'll use it."

I nod in agreement, but I'm not sure what he means. Use what? I'll have to think about it later.

Dad is pulling off his boots while I'm reading my letter to Stalin out loud. He smiles and tells me I wrote a good letter. He puts the letter into his briefcase and promises he'll deliver it. Then he says, "Your principal, Sergei Ivanych, called me at work today."

"Why? We don't have spies or enemies at school."

He looks at me sternly, and right away I know I lack in vigilance. "Can you say this with absolute certainty?" he asks.

I can't think of anyone who could be a spy or an enemy at school, but I say, "No, I can't."

He nods and hands me something wrapped in brown paper. "That's not why he called. Open it up."

Scarlet bursts out as I unwrap the package. The scarf of a Young Pioneer! The triangle of simple red cloth that every Pioneer must wear, but how beautiful it is and how long I have wished for it. Tomorrow, when I become a Pioneer, I will wear it for the first time.

I spread the scarf on the table, smooth the wrinkles, and say, "The three tips of the Pioneers scarf symbolize the union of three generations, mature Communists, the Communist Youth, and the Young Pioneers."

"Tell me why it's red," says my dad.

"The red color of the Pioneers scarf is the color of our Communist banner and represents blood spilled for the cause of the Communist Party!"

My dad nods and ties it around my neck just as the rule says—the right tip extending lower than the left—and says, "Young Pioneer! Ready to fight for the cause of the Communist Party and Comrade Stalin?"

I shoot my arm up in the Pioneers salute and reply, "Always ready!"

Here his face changes, and by the look he has now, I know what he's going to say.

"Your mother would be so proud," he says.

I see myself reflected in his glasses; scarlet burns at my throat. My hand goes up to it. After

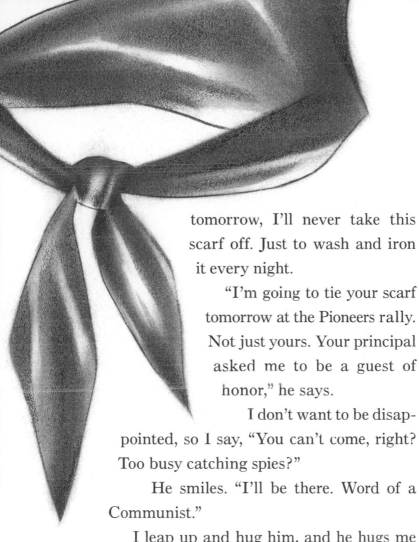

tomorrow, I'll never take this
scarf off. Just to wash and iron
it every night.

"I'm going to tie your scarf
tomorrow at the Pioneers rally.
Not just yours. Your principal
asked me to be a guest of
honor," he says.

I don't want to be disap-
pointed, so I say, "You can't come, right?
Too busy catching spies?"

He smiles. "I'll be there. Word of a
Communist."

I leap up and hug him, and he hugs me

back. He's so strong, my ribs are about to crack. Then he says quietly in my ear, "Anything ever happens to me, go to Aunt Larisa. She'll put you up."

Just then, our neighbor Orlov starts singing and playing his accordion.

Be calm, our Leader, we're standing guard.
We won't give the enemy even a yard.
Wherever we go, the world's set anew.
Life's getting better and happier too!

Dad sets me down, knocks on the wall, and says, "Keep it down, comrade. It's no time for parties."

Orlov stops right away; that is how much everybody respects my dad. He turns to me and says, "To bed, future Pioneer. Tomorrow's a big day."

I WAKE UP in the middle of the night, worried. Why did he say "Anything ever happens to me, go to Aunt Larisa"? I don't understand. What could happen to him?

I watch the faint shades of the falling snow slide across the ceiling, listening to his even breathing. After a while, I feel better. Nothing could happen to my dad; Stalin needs him.

I turn to the window, where a giant statue of Stalin gleams under searchlights. The statue is made from the steel of fighter planes and stands taller than

any building. You can see it from every window in Moscow.

Recently, my dad caught a gang of wreckers scheming to blow it up. Wreckers are enemies of the people and want to destroy our precious Soviet property. I can't imagine anybody who would dare to damage a monument to Comrade Stalin, but there are some bad characters out there. Obviously, they're always caught.

I stare at the statue and pretend it is Comrade
Stalin himself, watching over Moscow from his
great height. His steady eyes track a legion of shiny
black dots zipping up and down the snow-white
streets. The dots grow larger and larger, until they
turn into shiny black automobiles made of black
metal and bulletproof glass. These beautiful
machines belong to our State Security. I know

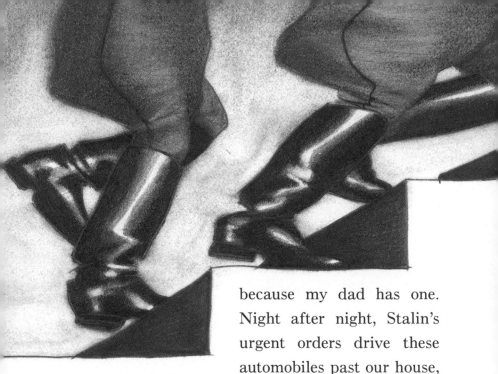

because my dad has one. Night after night, Stalin's urgent orders drive these automobiles past our house, but tonight one turns into our courtyard. I listen to the engine left running, doors slamming, and boots hurrying up the stairs. Then the doorbell rings.

This is how we know who has visitors—we count the rings. One for the Shulmans, two for the Ivanovs, three for the Stukachovs, four for the Kozlovs, five for us, and so on, all the way to the Lodochkins, who get twelve.

Ring, ring, ring, ring, ring.

Five. They want us.

Ring, ring, ring, ring, ring.

"Dad, Dad, a car for you. On Stalin's orders!"

Ring, ring, ring, ring, ring.

He sits up, wrapped in the sheet like a ghost, glares at me wildly, and says, "Stay in bed."

I wait till he leaves, then go after him into the kitchen. What I see in the dull glow of the room is the white sheet, taut and sweaty over his back. The front door is open; he's leaning out, listening to someone on the other side. When he finally turns, he has a face I've never seen before.

"What's wrong, Dad?"

Out of the darkness, three large figures in State Security uniforms stomp into the kitchen. They follow my dad past where I'm standing and into the corridor toward our room. The last in line catches his cap against the laundry line, picks it up, swears, and clomps after the rest. All this noise in the middle of the night, but our neighbors' doors stay shut. Nobody looks out to complain.

When I get to the room, Dad is sitting on the floor, holding his ear. The officer's leather belt creaks as he turns to look at me, his eyes bloodshot. "Nothing to worry about, little boy," he says in a hoarse voice. "A friendly chat, that's all."

The guards pull out the drawers and dump our things on the floor. They shake loose pages out of our books. They cut up Dad's mattress and feel inside it. They tap on the walls, listening for hidden places, and open part of the floor where the nails are loose. Soon what we have is in a pile, torn and wrecked. The only thing they don't touch is a framed picture of Stalin. But they look behind it.

My dad is still pulling on a shirt when the guards yank him out of the room. I grab his arm and hang on to him as tight as I can. This close, I see his ear is bleeding. "It's more important to join the Pioneers than to have a father," he whispers hurriedly. "You hear me?"

"No talking," orders the officer in his scratchy voice. "Move on." He shoves me aside.

In the corridor stands our neighbor Stukachov. "It's me, Stukachov. I made the report," he says, smiling and bobbing his head at the passing uniforms.

"Comrade Stalin appreciates your vigilance, citizen," says the officer, and without looking at Stukachov, he pushes on, my dad's briefcase under his arm. Then all of us together—the officer, the guards, my dad, Stukachov, and me, closing the rear—march down the corridor to the dimly lit kitchen. I notice we are walking in step. Left, right, left, right, left, right, like on parade.

"Comrade Senior Lieutenant?" calls Stukachov. "Regarding the boy?"

"The state will bring him up," says the officer. "They'll collect him first thing in the morning."

"Wise," Stukachov says. "We'll be moving in, then?"

The officer doesn't answer. Stukachov halts and I bump into him, and by the time I loop around and reach the front door, they are trotting down the steps.

"Dad! Dad! Wait!"

The officer spins and slams the front door shut with such force, I have to pull back fast so it won't smash my face. I try opening it, but the lock is jammed. I kick and kick, but the door won't budge. I dart to the window. Down below, the guards shove my dad into the car and slam the door. The engine revs up, tires spin in the snow, and, when the car leaps forward, the headlights blast across the windows. The icy glass before me flares up, turning white. When it's clear again, the courtyard is empty.

SOON THE COURTYARD turns blurry, warped at the edges. I rub at my eyes and my knuckles come away wet. Then I hear a broom sweeping the floor somewhere. I turn and listen. It's coming from our room.

When I get there, the door is open. Stukachov's wife is in our room, sweeping. What a good woman, rising from her sleep, helping to clean up.

"Move it, Vasya," she says. "They've changed their minds before."

I look into the room, and Stukachov is there,

too. He smiles at me briefly. He's piling our broken things on top of my dad's bedsheet, which is still stained with his sweat. Then he lifts the edges and ties the corners together. He takes the sack out and sets it in the corridor next to our other things, all broken. Then, as though I'm not there, they start moving their things into our room. Stukachov's mother comes in fast, carrying her pillow. It doesn't take them long to set up their furniture, make the beds, and bring their sleeping kids one by one and tuck them in.

It all happens so quickly, I don't even know yet how I feel about sharing our room with them. I start to walk in, but Stukachov blocks the door. I reach for the door handle, but his hand is clutching it. He leans in close. "Your daddy's been arrested," he says. "There's no room for you here."

I step back. He nods approvingly, steps into the

room, and closes the door. "He'll enjoy the orphan-age," he says to his wife. "All nice children."

The lock clicks.

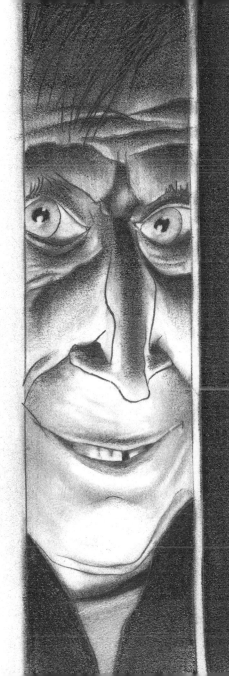

I'VE NEVER BEEN out alone in the middle of the night. A wind rattles the courtyard's gate as I peer into the dark street. Not a citizen in sight. I know there's nothing to be afraid of, and yet I don't go out there; I step back into the courtyard and look up at our dark window. The Stukachovs are sleeping, warm and cozy in our room. Tomorrow they'll throw away our broken things. That doesn't matter, of course. My dad and I oppose personal property on principle. Personal property will disappear when Communism comes. But still.

CHAPTER 7

I need to think things over. I could go back and sleep on the floor in the kitchen, next to the stove; I bet it's still warm after all the day's cooking. It's a large iron stove with twelve rings—one ring per family. After my mom died, we put a little Primus stove into our room for warming things up and gave our ring on the stove to the Stukachovs; with so many dependants to feed, they needed it more. Maybe that's what my dad meant when he said, "Don't talk to Stukachov. He'll use it." First we gave him the stove ring; now he's taken our room.

Maybe I don't need a room. Not everybody has one. Marfa Ivanovna doesn't have a room. She lives in a cubbyhole next to the toilet. Semenov sleeps behind the curtain in the corridor, and nobody's complaining. I feel better already. I'm staying in the kitchen until my dad returns.

Walking back to the door, I step over some tracks frozen into the snow. When I see these are the tire tracks from the car that took away my dad, I stop. Going back in that apartment is a weakness, not fit for a future Pioneer. They clearly arrested my dad by mistake. Wait till Stalin finds out.

But how long will it take before they tell Stalin? Stalin is busy; he has to take care of all of us, millions all over the country. And what if they don't tell him for a long time? Could be several days even. Who knows? My dad has to be at our Pioneers rally tomorrow by noon. There's no time to waste. I will tell Stalin myself.

RED SQUARE is deserted, layers of cobblestones under thick black ice. To go faster, I slide, my boots skimming over reflections of ruby stars that glow atop the Kremlin towers. The Kremlin is where Comrade Stalin's office is. Everybody knows his window—it's lit all night long. Our Leader works hard.

I imagine I'm there already, in Stalin's office. He is sitting behind his desk, smoking his pipe. "No time to lose, Comrade Stalin," I say. "My dad has been arrested!" He raises his eyebrows. He grabs the telephone. "Special unit! Emergency!" he says. "Wrench Zaichik's dad from the traitors' claws!"

But when the Kremlin guards see me, they run across the square, shouting and tugging at their sidearms. One slides on the ice and bumps into me. He swears, steam bursts out of his mouth, and he plunges his enormous mitten into my face. I duck

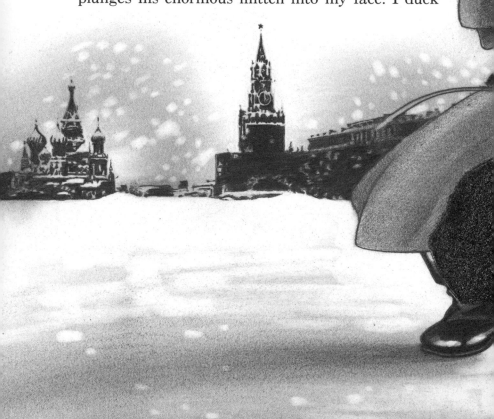

under and run. The guard blows a whistle and other whistles join in. Suddenly, guards are everywhere. One slips and falls, and his pistol goes off like a whip crack. At the far end of the square, a black automobile turns the corner, headlights slashing me in half.

I'M WINDED from running, so I take my time climbing the stairs. What was I thinking? That any fool could just walk into the Kremlin and talk to Stalin? With enemies everywhere and the international situation the way it is? Dad's right: I'm not serious enough. I don't think hard enough.

Aunt Larisa's apartment is on the fifth floor. When I get to her door, I stare at the nameplates under the buzzer; the number nine is scribbled next to her husband's name. I reach for the buzzer but don't touch it. I don't want her sitting up in bed, counting rings, wondering who has come for them in the middle of the night. I sit down on the step to catch my breath.

The door flies open and there's Aunt Larisa, holding a baby wrapped in a blanket. "I knew it," she whispers. "He's been arrested, right? Arrested?"

I stand up.

The baby starts crying and Aunt Larisa begins rocking it.

"Don't cry, baby. When you grow up, you'll be living in Communism," I say, and reach in to tickle the baby, but Aunt Larisa pulls it away, frightened. Then her husband is there, leaning out of the door.

"What are you trying to do, kid?" he says. "Get us in trouble?"

"I only need till morning," I say. "As soon as Stalin finds out, my dad is coming back."

"Stalin?" he says. He laughs, but it's a nasty laugh.

"It's not funny," I say. "I will be joining the Pioneers tomorrow and my dad is—"

"Forget about your dad, kid. Your dad's an
enemy of the people. Don't you get it? They don't
allow kids of enemies to join the Pioneers."

My aunt says something, but I can't hear it
because the baby is wailing.

"Shush!" her husband hisses, and I'm not sure
whom he's hissing at, my aunt or the baby, because
both are crying now. He leans forward and drives

his finger into my chest. "Don't aggravate us, kid. Get lost." And he shuts the door.

I'm almost at the first floor when I hear the door open upstairs. It's my aunt. I stop and wait for her to catch up. I knew she'd come, and she does, arms reaching out and pulling me in. With her face so close, I see she looks like my dad. Though my dad never cries, of course.

"He's wrong," I say. "My dad's not an enemy of the people. You know that, don't you?"

She nods and pats my head, or tries to arrange my hair—I don't know which. "I'm sorry, Sasha," she says. "If we take you in, they'll arrest us, too. We just had a baby. We have to stay alive."

She pushes something into the palm of my hand, folds my fingers over it, and runs upstairs. I know it's money. I'll need it, so I'm grateful. When I look, it's not much, but at least in the morning I can take a streetcar to school.

10

IN THE BASEMENT of my aunt's building, I find a stack of old newspapers. I set aside pages with Stalin's picture on them—don't want to damage those—and make a bed under the warm pipes. It's not so bad in here. The basement is cozy.

I think of the time I last saw Aunt Larisa. It was before she married that jerk. Dad dropped me off and said he would be taking Mom to the hospital because she was ill. I stayed in Aunt Larisa's room for two days. I didn't even go to school. When Dad came back, he said Mom had died at the hospital. I started crying, and Aunt Larisa hugged me and

said to my dad, "You look guilty, not sad." He didn't say anything, just took me home. There must have been a funeral. I wonder why he didn't take me. I need to ask him about that.

The pipes gurgle and hiss above me. In one of the apartments, someone turns on a record player. Normally I only listen to marching music, but this song I like. It's pretty and gentle. Why did Aunt Larisa say my dad looked guilty? He didn't. He looked sad. He blamed himself for not being able to save my mom. He's not even a doctor, but he's that responsible.

CHAPTER 10

I pull the newspapers over my head and start thinking about tomorrow. Tomorrow everything will be better. Tomorrow Stalin will rescue my dad. Tomorrow I will be a Pioneer. I drift off and dream of the Pioneers rally and see my dad, who's smiling and tying the Pioneers scarf around my neck.

THE SOUND of someone scraping ice in the courtyard wakes me. A small window above my head glows bright with winter-morning light.

I dash up the stairs, through the front door, and out into the street. The sidewalks are crowded. Citizens rush to work, line up for food rations, push into the streetcars. On the corner, a loudspeaker blares our country's anthem. They always play it at 8:45 sharp, which means I am late for school.

I chase after a streetcar white with frost, icicles hanging over the frozen windows. The streetcar is gaining speed, screeching over icy tracks. I manage

to hop on, but the streetcar is so crammed with passengers, I can't squeeze inside. I grab on to the railing and hang outside the doors. The streetcar bounces and darts forward, moving faster and faster, careening down the sloping street. Freezing air lashes my face as Moscow flies by in a whirlwind. After all the bad things that happened last night, this crazy ride is so exciting and fun that I start laughing.

BY THE TIME I get to school, it's snowing again. Everybody's out in the school yard flinging snowballs. I love snowball fights. I have three marksmanship awards from the war-preparedness class, so everyone wants me on their team. I join in. Soon my team is on the offensive, but, of course, Vovka Sobakin has to spoil it. "Watch out, *Amerikanetz*!" he yells, and rams into me so hard, we fly into a snowdrift. He calls me *Amerikanetz* on account of my mother. Vovka used to be my best friend, but I shouldn't have told him anyway. My dad warned me never to tell anyone.

"Stop pawing me," I say to Vovka, push him

aside, and walk away. When I hear him yell "Death to the enemy of the people!" I freeze. Does he know about my dad? I turn around just as Vovka is lifting a snowball, but he doesn't throw it at me. He throws it at Four-Eyes. Several kids join Vovka and line up into a firing squad. They hurl snowballs at Four-Eyes, who's backed against a wall. He doubles over and covers his face to protect his glasses.

Four-Eyes is Borka Finkelstein, the only Jewish kid in our class. His parents were arrested at the beginning of the year and now he lives with his relatives. We call him Four-Eyes because he wears eyeglasses. Anybody who's not a worker or a peasant and reads a lot, we call Four-Eyes. And it's true; Finkelstein reads a lot.

"Hit him, *Amerikanetz*!" Vovka tries to force the snowball into my hand. The snowball is icy hard and would hurt. I don't feel like throwing it.

"Comrades, look!" Vovka yells. "Zaichik refuses to shoot the enemy!"

"Traitor!" someone shouts. "Enemy of the people!"

"Who's not with us is against us," Vovka says, grinning, and holds up the snowball. Everyone stares at me, waiting to see what I'll do. That's when Four-Eyes decides to take a chance and throw a snowball. He's nearly blind, so it's a fluke, but it hits me on the ear. Everyone laughs. Before I know what I'm doing, I grab the snowball from Vovka's hand and throw it at Four-Eyes. There's a loud pop as it hits him in the face. The eyeglasses snap, glass splinters, and one shard cuts his cheek.

MY DESK IS FRONT and center, right next to the desk of Nina Petrovna, our classroom teacher. She always seats the best pupils up front. Vovka Sobakin used to sit in my place, but now he's in the back, in Kolyma, with all the bad ones. We call the back row Kolyma because Kolyma is a faraway region in our country where Stalin sends those who don't deserve to live and work among the honest people.

Vovka used to be our model student—first to finish tests, never a grade below an A, helping those lagging behind. Vovka had exceptional penmanship and was also a talented artist. When he won the art competition, our principal hung Vovka's drawing, *Comrade Stalin at the Helm*, in the main hall. But one day, Vovka snapped. Nobody knows what happened, but he dropped to the bottom of the class academically and started getting reported for bad behavior. Vovka's drawing disappeared from the main hall.

"I have an important announcement, children," says Nina Petrovna. "The Communist hero, the eagle eyes of our beloved State Security, and the father of your classmate, our dear comrade Zaichik, will be attending the Pioneers rally today and will personally tie the scarves on all of our new Pioneers. Isn't it wonderful?"

I feel everybody's eyes on me, so I sit up the way Nina Petrovna always tells us to: arms folded, back straight, looking up at her. I hope I don't look nervous. The rally is at noon, during the main recess. Will my dad be on time? I don't know. Did someone already tell Stalin? I'm sure someone did;

our State Security is well organized. By now, Stalin must have sent his order: "Free Zaichik immediately!" It's such a simple thing, and Stalin is a brilliant genius of humanity. They always say it on the radio.

"You'll be joining today, Zaichik," says Nina Petrovna, smiling her nicest smile at me. "Would you be so kind as to recite for us the Laws of the Young Soviet Pioneers? Children, listen carefully and repeat after Zaichik."

I stand up. I say, loud and clear, "The Young Pioneer is devoted to Comrade Stalin, the Communist Party, and Communism."

Just as everyone starts repeating, Nina Petrovna raises her hand for all to stop and says in a stern voice, "Sobakin, what are you doing? Do not repeat after Zaichik. You know perfectly well you're not to be accepted."

Vovka shrugs. Nina Petrovna smiles at me. "Continue, Zaichik."

"A Young Pioneer is a reliable comrade and always acts according to conscience."

"Up, Sobakin!" calls Nina Petrovna. "How dare you repeat the sacred laws after Zaichik? Into the corner, criminal!"

That's the way our Nina Petrovna is. She's nice and fair, but when necessary, she's firm. In my opinion, she's the best teacher in our school.

Vovka slides off his chair and hobbles to the wall, making crazy faces. Everyone laughs.

"Face the wall, Sobakin," says Nina Petrovna. She turns to me and smiles again, but I see she's angry. Her face is all purple. "I'm sorry, Zaichik. I promise there'll be no more interruptions. Please continue."

She's keeping her eye on Vovka, ready to correct him, but Vovka's quiet, so I keep going. I've had these laws down since I was six. When I get to "A Young Pioneer has a right to criticize shortcomings," the door opens and Four-Eyes shuffles in. I should have had more self-control and stopped myself before I threw that snowball at him. Four-Eyes's glasses are gone and he holds a bloodied kerchief to his cheek. Everyone laughs.

"What a pleasant surprise, Finkelstein," says Nina Petrovna. "A stellar example of another individual who will not be permitted to join the Pioneers." Then she glares at Vovka and says, "Sobakin's work, no doubt."

"I didn't do it."

"Don't expect me to believe you," snaps Nina Petrovna. "Finkelstein? What happened to you?"

Four-Eyes squints at her and his body starts swaying a little.

"Stop rocking back and forth, Finkelstein. You're not in a synagogue."

Everyone laughs.

"Speak, Finkelstein."

He doesn't.

"Pay attention, children. We are learning a

valuable lesson. In our country, even the children of enemies are allowed a choice—cooperate or face the consequences."

She looks at us significantly. "Finkelstein refuses to cooperate with authority, which is me, the teacher. In capitalist countries, the teacher would decide whether to admit Finkelstein back into the classroom or send him to the principal to receive his punishment. But remember, children, the Soviet classroom

is the most democratic in the world. You will decide his fate. You will vote. Those in favor of sending Finkelstein to the principal, raise your hands."

All hands pop up.

Nina Petrovna turns to me and I see that she's surprised. "Are you undecided, Zaichik, or against?"

"He did it. He broke his glasses," says Vovka into the wall.

"Not another word out of you, Sobakin, or you will be on your way to the principal, as well. Our Zaichik is an example of dedication. He is the son of a hero. Nothing like you."

She walks up to me, puts her hands on my shoulders, and looks me straight in the eye. "I have submitted a request to select you as a banner-bearer at today's Pioneers rally, Zaichik. Imagine how proud your father will be, seeing you carrying our red banner into the main hall." Then she makes a sad face and sighs. "Of course, I may have to withdraw my request. We don't allow those who vote against the majority to handle the sacred banner. You're a smart boy, Zaichik; you understand."

Hands still raised, everyone stares at me.

"What will it be, Sasha?" she says quietly. "For or against?"

I raise my hand.

14

THE STORAGE ROOM is in the basement. I knock on the door, but it doesn't open, so I knock again. Matveich, the janitor, is half deaf, and I bet he's sleeping now. Some people are just ignorant; they slow down our march toward Communism. I knock louder. I'll knock for as long as it takes—Nina Petrovna sent me here to get the banner, so I'm not leaving without it.

Finally, Matveich opens the door a crack and looks out at me suspiciously. He never allows anybody into the storage room. I wonder what he's hiding in there. I hand him the teacher's request and he stares at it, moving his lips.

"Who signed this?" he says.

"Nina Petrovna."

"Doesn't look it. Where's the stamp?"

"What stamp?"

"The chief's stamp, what else? Anybody can just show up here. The rules say, no stamp—no drums, no bugles, and no banner. This is serious business. It's state property we're talking about."

I'm changing my mind about Matveich. He's not all bad. He's vigilant. I take the request back from him and fly upstairs to the principal's office. I have to hurry. Nina Petrovna has already started practicing for the rally. The carrying of the banner is the most important part.

Outside the principal's office sits Four-Eyes, still waiting. The worst thing is, he smiles at me.

"Sorry about your glasses," I say.

He shrugs. "Why does Vovka call you *Amerikanetz*?"

I shouldn't tell him. "My mom was American. Don't tell anyone."

He squints at me. "And she was arrested and shot?"

"What do you mean? Of course not. She came from America to help us build Communism."

He nods. "They think all foreigners are spies."

"She wasn't a spy! She was a real Communist."

"My mom and dad are real Communists, too," Four-Eyes says. "They are in Lubyanka prison now—enemies of the people."

I look away. Lubyanka prison is on the bottom floor of the State Security building. My dad's office sits above it.

"My aunt took me there last week," says Four-Eyes. "We stood in line for two days, but when we got to the door, they wouldn't let us see them. No visitation rights, they said. My aunt tells me they always say this when the prisoners have been shot already, but I know she's lying. They're alive and I'm going to see them." He leans in, grabs my arm, and whispers fast. "You can get inside. Your dad works there. All I need is somebody to distract the guards. What do you say, Zaichik? I'd do it for you if your dad were locked up."

I pull my arm away so fast, he tumbles to the floor. When I try to help him, he pushes me away. He gets up on the bench, leans back, and squints at me, smiling. "It's all right. I'll get in by myself."

Four-Eyes is crazy.

MATVEICH SQUEEZES the banner through the crack in the door and says, "Keep it wrapped."

I didn't know the banner would be this heavy, but the weight makes it even more important. I heave it onto my shoulder, climb two sets of stairs, and enter the main hall. The hall is deserted now; everyone's in class. I know I shouldn't, but I untie the cord and turn the pole until the heavy cloth, decked in gold fringe, unfurls. The banner is beautiful. Comrade Stalin's profile, embroidered in gold thread against the color of blood shed for the cause

of the Communist Party, shines under the curved Pioneers motto, Always Ready.

At the end of the hall, a plaster statue of Comrade Stalin is set between two windows. Not a full statue, just chest and head, no arms even. But it looks real; I feel like Stalin himself is looking at me. I lift up the banner and, swirling the pole so that the cloth whooshes above my head, march toward him.

As I march, I imagine the parade on May Day, my favorite day of the year. I hear the crashing brass of a marching band and I see crowds of people applauding and waving red flags and shouting, "Long live Comrade Stalin!" Under my feet, the ground rumbles as the mighty Red Army tanks roll onto Red Square, and up above, a formation of fighter planes, flying in a cloudless sky, shapes six giant letters: S-T-A-L-I-N.

I wish my dad could see me now; he'd be so proud. Already a Pioneer, I'm riding atop a parade

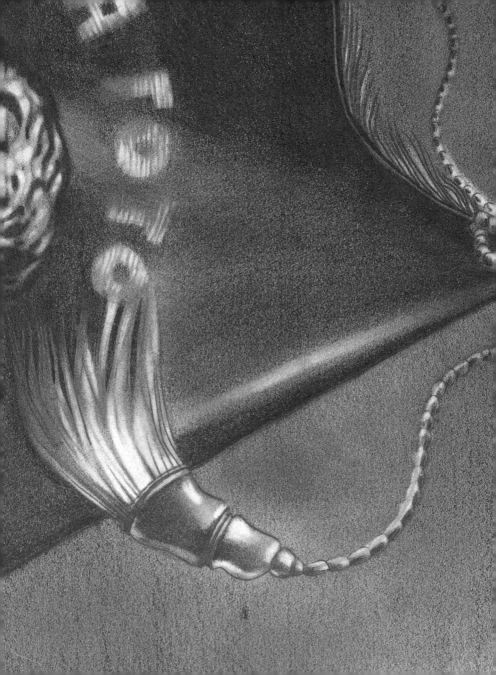

float all decked in crimson and gold. I hold the banner as high as I can and I stare straight ahead, and what I see is our radiant Communist future. I can't describe it, but I believe it's there. Believing is the most important part. If you really believe in something, it will come true.

The float rolls by the marble mausoleum from where Stalin, our great Leader and Teacher, watches the parade with his generals. He waves at me, his eyes twinkling kindly. "This is what we are fighting for, comrades. This Young Pioneer is our Communist future. What is your name, son?"

"My name is Sasha Zaichik, Comrade Stalin," I shout from my float. "You awarded my dad the order of the Red Banner and called him 'an iron broom purging the vermin from our midst.'"

"Ah, Zaichik." Stalin nods, smiling. "I know him well, a hero and a devoted Communist."

"A terrible mistake has been made, Comrade Stalin," I yell. "My dad has been arrested!"

What comes next has never happened on any May Day before. The parade starts moving backward. Not just moving. People are running, trying to get away from Comrade Stalin's powerful voice thundering across Red Square. "Spies! Traitors! Enemies of the people! Who made this mistake? Who's responsible? Arrest them! Arrest them all!"

The float vanishes from under my feet. I tumble into the crowd. A stampede of panicked citizens sweeps me away and soon I lose sight of the mausoleum. I clutch the banner to my chest, but then—I don't know how—I'm not at Red Square anymore. I'm back in my school's main hall, running headlong into the statue of Stalin. The banner shoots out of my hands and its pointy metal tip knocks Stalin's plaster nose clean off his face.

THE PLASTER DUST sparkles in the muted window light before landing on the floor around the nose. I look at the broken nose. I look at the banner, spread nearby. Then I look up at Stalin, now without a nose. It doesn't take much to know what will happen next.

First, I will never become a Pioneer. Second, the principal will telephone the State Security to report an act of terrorism in his school. Third, everybody will find out who did it. Next, the guards will arrive to arrest me. It won't be a mistake like with my dad;

CHAPTER 16

I should be arrested. Son of a hero and a Communist, I have become an enemy of the people, a wrecker. I have damaged our precious Soviet property. No, more than that. I have defaced a sacred statue of Stalin. Not on purpose, of course; it was an accident—I lost hold of the banner. It could have happened to anyone. But who's going to believe me? Nobody saw how it happened.

Just then, a shadow passes over the nose. The sound of footsteps. I turn around, but no one is there. At that moment, the school bell explodes. In a second, the classroom doors will burst open and kids will run out and see what I've done. I leap up, grab the banner, and sprint for the closest door—the boys' toilets.

THE STALLS DON'T have doors, but I still dash into the farthest one to stay out of view. I stand next to the toilet, making sure the banner isn't touching the wet floor. My heart's pounding. Everyone's already in the main hall, the laughing and shrieking and stomping so loud, the floor trembles. Or is it my knees?

This is the last recess before the rally in which I was to become a Pioneer. I feel the Pioneers scarf my dad gave me folded neatly in my chest pocket, right over my heart. The scarf is the only thing I took from the apartment. I close my eyes and say in my head, *Dear Comrade Stalin, I'm very sorry I broke your nose. You know how much I love you. You know how much I want to be a Pioneer. Please make it so I can become one. Please. I'll be your best Pioneer, I promise.*

Just as I say that, the noise outside stops. Someone giggles, then stifles the giggle. Someone runs up the stairs. The door bangs, and suddenly it is Nina Petrovna's voice. "Step back, children! Step back! Immediately return to your classrooms!"

The decision comes instantly. This is what I'm going to do: follow Nina Petrovna's order. She sent me to get the banner. I got it. What happened on the way back, I can't change. I will answer for that when the time comes. For now, I'm taking the banner back into the classroom. I try to wrap the banner, but my hands are shaking. I keep at it and in the end it wraps perfectly, tight and smooth, not a crease. I take a deep breath, heave the banner over my shoulder, and reach for the door, when it bursts open. Vovka Sobakin, who else? He grabs the banner out of my hands and jabs it around like a rifle with a bayonet attached. It's a drill we learned in our war-preparedness class.

"So immature, Sobakin," I say, trying to sound calm. "Hand it back."

He jabs me in the stomach, but I'm not letting him provoke me. The Pioneers rules are clear on this: no fights. Next he starts jabbing at the walls.

"Sobakin, I'm warning you. This banner is state property. You'll damage it."

He doesn't care. He drops the sacred Pioneers banner right down on the wet floor and looks at me with eyes so scary, I step back.

"Destruction or damage of state property shall be punishable by the supreme measure of social defense—proclaiming the guilty an enemy of the people and shooting by the firing squad," he says. "Criminal Code of the Soviet Union, Article 58."

"What?"

"Are you stupid or just pretending? You think you're not going to pay for this?" he says. "Forget about the Pioneers, *Amerikanetz*. I saw you." He pulls Stalin's plaster nose out of his pocket.

"CHILDREN, WHAT is our duty as future Pioneers?" says Nina Petrovna. "It is to collectively expose those responsible for what happened to Comrade Stalin's statue. Then and only then will we be allowed to proceed with the Pioneers rally. Act in the Stalinist spirit and you will earn the red Pioneers scarf tied around your neck."

Everyone is quiet. Nina Petrovna scans the classroom.

"Now take out your pencils," she says. "On a new sheet of paper, write down the names of the pupils in our class whom you suspect might be responsible. When finished, sign and date your list in the upper right corner and pass it to the front."

Nobody moves.

"Children? Why are we not writing?"

"We're not sure, Nina Petrovna." It's Zina Krivko; she always speaks for everybody.

"How can you not be sure, Zina? Did you do it?"

"No."

"Do you think your friend Tamara did it?"

Zina looks at her desk partner, Tamara. Tamara turns white. Zina turns back to Nina Petrovna and shakes her head.

"See, Zina, it's simple. You know who didn't do it," says Nina Petrovna. "I'll make it easy for you. Write down the names of the pupils who you're sure didn't do it."

Relieved, Zina lifts a pencil, bends over her workbook, covers it with her other hand so nobody can copy, and scribbles away.

"Good, Zina. Keep going," says Nina Petrovna,

watching her for a moment. "Just make sure you are right. You know what will happen if even one name on your list turns out to be unreliable?"

Zina shakes her head. She doesn't know.

"You, yourself, will be suspected," says Nina Petrovna. "We'll know that Zina Krivko is covering for the enemies of the people."

Zina pulls away from her workbook. The tip of her pencil starts tapping the paper. *Tap, tap, tap.* I see that her hand is shaking.

Nina Petrovna looks at her, surprised. "What's wrong, Zina? Why did you stop writing?"

Zina opens and closes her mouth several times before she can speak again. "I'm not sure who's reliable, Nina Petrovna," she says quietly.

"That's it, Zina," says Nina Petrovna. "The ones who you're not sure are reliable are the suspicious ones. Those are the names you want to write down. Understand?"

Nina Petrovna looks up at the class. "Children, does everyone understand?"

I hear people shifting in their seats and soon pencils start to scribble. I look over my shoulder at Vovka. He's grinning at me and pretending to sharpen his pencil with a knife. When I turn back, Nina Petrovna stands in front of my desk.

"Sasha? You're not writing?"

I wish I had some excuse—that I didn't have any paper or that my pencil needed sharpening—but there's paper in front of me, pencil sharp as always.

"Sasha?" she says, this time louder. "Write at least one name, Sasha. Should be easy to guess, shouldn't it?"

She looks over my head and now I see she is staring at Vovka. She stares long and hard, making sure we all know who she's looking at.

"Can you spell your own name, Sobakin?" she says. "Write it down."

I turn to look at Vovka. Everyone does. Vovka's desk scrapes the floor as he rises, clenching his fists. What is he going to do? Hit Nina Petrovna? By the look of him, he would. But nothing happens. The door opens and Matveich pokes his head in. "All classes to the cafeteria. Chief's orders."

19

"A WAVE OF ANGER and profound outrage engulfed the entire body of our school when we uncovered the unspeakably monstrous crime that took place in the main hall. Undeniably, a group of filthy and cowardly conspirators, spies, murderers, and provocateurs has infiltrated our school. These heinous degenerates, these traitors to the Motherland, aim to undermine . . . "

The principal, Sergei Ivanych, stops hollering to clear his throat. Then he stands there a moment, holding on to the podium, wheezing. He starts again. Sergei Ivanych is a dedicated Communist and I'm always in agreement with his speeches, but this time he's gone too far. I should know. I'm the only one who knows what really happened. Hold on—I'm not the only one; Vovka knows, too. I turn around and look at the back of the crowd—that's where he'd be—but he's not there. Matveich locked the cafeteria doors. Nobody's allowed to leave. So where is he? Vovka is up to something bad again, definitely.

"But the spies miscalculated. Our fearless, keen-eyed State Security will spoil their plans, unmask the pack of terrorists, and catch them red-handed!" Sergei Ivanych strikes the podium. "Without mercy we'll sweep off the face of the earth this nest of treachery and filth!"

My classmate Anton shoves me in the back. "Zaichik, your dad's here."

I push myself up so I can see through the window that opens onto the street. Anton's right. A black State Security automobile slides up to the entrance. It must be him. He gave me the word of a Communist and he's kept it. *Thank you, Comrade Stalin. Thank you for helping my dad to keep his word.*

"He's coming to the Pioneers rally," says Anton, giggling. "Maybe he can catch the wreckers."

I wait for the black doors to open, but when I see who steps out of the car, I turn away from the window fast. It's not my dad at all. It is the senior lieutenant who arrested my dad last night.

WHEN THE SENIOR lieutenant and his guards enter the cafeteria, Sergei Ivanych yells, "Spontaneous applause, everybody!" He claps wildly, until the teachers start clapping; then the rest of us join in, and we all clap for a long time. I wonder if this is what the newspapers mean when they say "a prolonged standing ovation." Does it count if we were already standing when they came in?

Sergei Ivanych nods to Dubasov, our physical education teacher. Dubasov dives behind the curtain and instantly returns with a wooden crate overflowing with loose sheets of paper. We all know what those are. Every class had to write a list of suspects of who might have broken off Stalin's nose. Dubasov sets the crate before the senior lieutenant and salutes him like a soldier. Sergei Ivanych waves him off and Dubasov darts out of the way, embarrassed. The lieutenant doesn't even look at the box. We are still applauding when he unbuckles his holster, pulls out his pistol, and points it at the ceiling. The cafeteria turns dead silent right away.

He slips the pistol back into the holster. His eyes search the crowd, but his head doesn't move. I shift to where I think he won't see me, but I can't be sure; those eyes look like they see through walls.

"Whoever chipped the nose off the statue will now raise his hand," he says quietly, but somehow everyone can hear, even in the back. I know this is when I should come clean, raise my hand, and confess right here in front of everybody. *Forget about becoming a Pioneer, Sasha Zaichik. Raise your hand. Raise your hand now.* I know this is what I should do, but I hesitate, and somebody else's hand pops up to the left of the stage.

The crowd gasps and heaves back, and there stands Four-Eyes Finkelstein, holding his hand up. The lieutenant frowns and nods to the guards. They cut through the crowd, lift Four-Eyes under the arms, and carry him to the exit. When they pass by where I'm standing, the crazy kid winks at me.

WE WALK FROM the cafeteria in pairs, holding hands. Talking is not allowed. I take the time to think about Four-Eyes.

We all saw the guards shoving him into the car. They did it the same way—doubling him over and pushing him in—as they had done to my dad last night. Now, squeezed between the guards, Four-Eyes is riding to Lubyanka prison, probably smiling his crazy smile at them. Why did he do it? Why did he take the blame for something he didn't do?

I imagine the car stopping at Lubyanka's gates, the guard stepping up, looking inside. He studies

Four-Eyes, waves the gates open. Is Four-Eyes scared? He must be scared, wondering what will happen inside. Nothing will happen, of course; he's just a kid. Kid or not, they'll probably search him for concealed weapons. They won't find anything. What can they find? A snowball? Then they'll take his clothes away and give him prisoner's pajamas. Prisoner's pajamas always have stripes on them. They will probably be too big for him; I doubt they have kids' sizes in there. Then the guards will lock him in a prison cell. Will he be alone, or will there be others in the cell? What if there are real criminals in there? What if they are enemies of the people? Spies and wreckers? What if my dad is in there, too? No, that's impossible. They don't lock a hero in a cell. But Finkelstein's dad could be there. His mom is probably in the women's quarters. His dad could be sitting in that cell, all worried, when the door opens and his son walks in. That'd be something to see.

I stop walking. People bump into me and the ranks get confused. "Keep in line, children, keep in line!" calls Nina Petrovna. Someone punches me in the back and I fall in with everybody again.

How stupid of me! I should have guessed it right away. Four-Eyes took the blame so he would be taken to Lubyanka. What a clever guy! He figured out how to get inside. He did exactly what he wanted, and I helped him. Well, not directly. But it doesn't matter now. Imagine how happy he'll be to see his dad, and how happy his dad will be to see him! I wonder if they have prison cells for whole families. Tonight they could be together, talking away. And who knows, maybe his parents are not enemies of the people after all. Maybe they were arrested by mistake, like my dad. Soon Stalin will let them all go. And if not, Four-Eyes is clever; he'll think of something.

Nina Petrovna holds the classroom door open and we file in. She pats each passing head, counting.

I smile at her—I can't help it. By the look on her face, I know the Pioneers rally is back on track. Soon I will see my dad. Soon I will become a Pioneer. Soon everything will be good again. But just as I'm getting in, Vovka Sobakin jumps out from behind the door and slams me into the wall. "Nice work, *Amerikanetz.*" His face is so close, his spit is all over me. "Let others take the blame. That's the Pioneer spirit."

22

"AS THE PROVERB goes, the apple doesn't fall far from the tree," says Nina Petrovna, looking out at us from behind her desk. "We should have known better than to permit Finkelstein to remain in our ranks after his parents were arrested. We have failed, class, slackened in our vigilance. But this will not happen again."

Nina Petrovna rises, walks to where the group photograph of our class hangs on the wall, and blackens Four-Eyes's face with her ink pen. That's what we always do to the pictures of enemies of the people, and it usually feels good, but not this time.

Four-Eyes is not an enemy. He just wanted to see his parents.

Satisfied now, Nina Petrovna turns away from the picture. She says, "Thanks to Finkelstein, we have very little time left to prepare for the Pioneers rally. But will this stop us from doing an excellent job?"

"No!" we yell.

"That's the Pioneer spirit, children. Drums and bugles, line up by the blackboard. Zaichik, bring the banner."

We line up in a flash, eager for Nina Petrovna's next command, but for some reason she's staring at the class photograph again. I look at it, too. The black ink glistens, still wet on Four-Eyes's face. When Nina Petrovna turns around, she looks serious and determined. "Children," she says, "your teacher has a confession to make."

Everyone gets really quiet; we've never heard a teacher confess to the students before.

"For some time, and contrary to my Stalinist

principles," she says, "I have been forced by my superior to keep silent." Here she looks up at the principal's office, right above our classroom; then she looks back at us significantly, making sure that we understand she's talking about our principal. "But in view of the vicious act of terrorism that happened in our school today, I refuse to be silenced any longer. Listen carefully, children. This is something I should have told you before." She takes a deep breath and says, "We have another individual in this class who is a child of the enemy of the people."

My dad always tells me to breathe through my nose if I choke on something. This way, you won't suffocate. But this is worse than choking—I can't breathe at all, not even through my nose. I glance at the door, judging the distance. If I run to it, she won't be able to stop me. But I don't run. Nina Petrovna says, "Sasha Zaichik!" and points her finger at me. Then everybody cranes his neck to take a good look at the child of an enemy of the people. I squeeze my eyes shut. Suddenly, the weight of the banner I'm holding is unbearable. In the next moment, it hits the floor.

"Pick up the banner, Zaichik," Nina Petrovna says calmly. I open my eyes. Nina Petrovna is not even looking at me. It was all in my imagination. She's facing the back of the class, her finger aimed at Vovka instead. "Sobakin, why don't you tell us what your father was accused of? Wrecking, wasn't it?"

People gasp and turn to gape at Vovka. Someone whistles. When I finally look myself, Vovka is rising from his seat slowly, drilling into Nina Petrovna with the same scary eyes he turned on me in the boys' toilets.

"You should know, children, that Sobakin's father was executed as an enemy of the people," says Nina Petrovna. "Does it explain his hideous anti-Soviet behavior and the likely fact he was conspiring with Finkelstein? What do you think, children?"

Before anyone has time to answer, Vovka flies at

Nina Petrovna, grips her by the throat, and begins strangling her. Nina Petrovna's face turns red and her eyes bulge. She makes gurgling noises and starts kicking up her legs. Nina Petrovna and Vovka knock things to the floor and bump into desks.

Everybody jumps up; some are screaming, but most are laughing. I know the Pioneers never get involved in fights, but before I know what I'm doing, I join in and try to separate them. Now there are three of us stumbling and grunting and bumping into desks for what seems like a long time, until somebody runs out to fetch Matveich and the others. Soon they are dragging Vovka and me off to the principal's office, with Nina Petrovna staggering behind and sobbing.

23

WE ARE TOLD to wait while the principal talks to Nina Petrovna. They argue behind the closed door, her hoarse voice barely a whisper. I wonder if she sounds like this from Vovka's trying to strangle her. We are waiting on the same bench that I saw Four-Eyes sitting on just this morning. This morning when I came here to get the principal's signature, he was planning to get into Lubyanka to see his parents, sitting in exactly the same spot I'm sitting in now. I wonder if he's with his dad already.

I steal a glance at Vovka. "Sorry about your

dad," I say. He doesn't even look at me. He sits there, chewing on his nails.

I understand how he must feel. If my dad were shot, wouldn't I be angry? What's hard to believe is this: Vovka's dad, an enemy of the people? When Vovka and I were friends, I went to his apartment hundreds of times. I liked his dad. He was a good Soviet citizen, modest, a devoted Communist. How could he be a wrecker? I start thinking about it but get nowhere. It's just too confusing. Then I remember what my dad used to say: "There's no smoke without a fire." If someone is arrested and executed, there must be a good reason for it. The State Security wouldn't be shooting people for nothing. What about my dad, then? He was arrested.

"Sobakin! Zaichik! Get in here!" the principal yells from his office.

I get up, but Vovka doesn't move. I feel bad for him, so I pat him on the shoulder, urging him to join me. Out of the blue, he leaps up and grabs me by the collar. "I was this close to strangling that teacher scum if not for you. Trying to be a hero like your perfect dad? Too late, dirty wrecker. I'm turning you in."

He shoves me aside and strides into the office. In the doorway, he bumps into Nina Petrovna, who is walking out; she shrieks and leaps back. Vovka gives her a nasty grin and goes in. I wait for Nina Petrovna to exit, but she doesn't, glaring at me suspiciously. Sergei Ivanych yells again, "Get in, criminals; I don't have all day." Nina Petrovna darts out and I go in. Sergei Ivanych orders me to lock the door and stand next to Vovka by the wall.

It's bright daylight outside, but his office is dark. All I can see are the large portrait of Stalin and, below, Sergei Ivanych at his desk, eyeing us angrily. "Let me explain what we are looking at," he says. "I'll make it simple." He looks at Vovka.

"First you, Sobakin. Thanks to you, I'll have to answer to the appropriate authorities for my weakness of character. No telling what they'll do. I let you stay after your father was put away and I kept it quiet, but what do you do? You attack Nina Petrovna."

"She's scum," Vovka says.

"I didn't hear it, Sobakin." He turns to me. "You, Zaichik. Your father has been arrested and locked up in Lubyanka. You think I don't know?"

I press my back against the wall to keep from falling.

He goes on: "So why not come to me and say, 'Sergei Ivanych, I want to purify myself from the rotten influence of my father. I want to march with my school to where great Stalin leads.' Huh? You didn't do that, did you?"

I can feel Vovka staring at me, but I won't turn my head.

"Had you done that," Sergei Ivanych says, "I would have let you denounce your father at today's Pioneers rally. Who knows, maybe we'd even have let you join the Pioneers. But no, you chose to pretend that you are still one of us."

Here he slams his fist against the desktop so hard, his phone receiver flies off the cradle. "You think you can get away from our State Security? They've been calling all day from the orphanage

for the children of the enemies of the people. What was
I supposed to tell them, that
you're not here?"

Only when Vovka grabs me under my arm do I notice that I'm sliding down to the floor.

"Sobakin," says Sergei Ivanych, "pull up a chair for Zaichik. The boy needs to sit down."

I drop into the chair Vovka brings. I guess my dad is not coming to the rally after all. Not coming after all.

Sergei Ivanych sighs, sits back, and looks at us not unkindly. "Boys, boys, you don't know what's good for you," he says. "Finally, we got rid of that Jew, Finkelstein. That might have satisfied the authorities for a while. But no, you had to get in trouble. I'm sending you both to the orphanage. Case closed."

"Finkelstein didn't do it," Vovka says.

"Not my problem. He confessed." Sergei Ivanych shuffles papers on his desk, then looks up at Vovka. "How do you know he didn't do it?"

"Don't send me to the orphanage and I'll tell you."

"Don't you blackmail me, Sobakin. You know who broke off the nose?"

"I do," Vovka says.

Sergei Ivanych smiles. "Here's a chance to correct our failures." He reaches for the phone. "Operator, get me State Security," he says into the receiver; then he looks up at me and says, "Think you can make it back to class, Zaichik?"

I nod.

"Run along," he says. "I'll deal with you later."

24

IN THE MAIN HALL, the statue I damaged has been hauled away. It must have been heavy; there are gashes in the floor where they dragged Stalin to the staircase. I wonder where they've taken it. I look around. The hall is deserted, just as it was this morning when I marched in bearing the banner, imagining the May Day parade. It seems like ages ago.

In no hurry to get back to Nina Petrovna's class, I dawdle in the corridor, listening to the sounds coming from behind the closed doors. The classes are in progress. I hear teachers' voices, feet marching to an accordion, chalk knocking against a blackboard, someone practicing a bugle. Everyone is learning to be useful to our country. Everyone is marching toward Communism, everyone but me. I am no longer a part of the Communist "WE."

This is a new feeling, and I don't like it, but it's better not to think about it. This new feeling, I decide, will go away by itself. To distract myself, I peek in on the Russian literature class, not particularly my favorite. The portraits of dead writers line the walls. They all have beards. Luzhko, a substitute teacher, stands at the blackboard. He also has a beard.

"What is the profound meaning of this masterpiece of Russian literature?" he says to the class. "Why is 'The Nose' still so important to us?"

No hands go up, and I'm not surprised. He's talking about a crazy old story they always make us read, called "The Nose." It's really stupid. Some guy's nose is dressed up in uniform—imagine that!—and it starts putting on airs, as though it's an important government official. It takes place way before Stalin was our Leader and Teacher, of course. Could something like this happen now? No way. So why should Soviet children read such lies? I don't know. I'm in no hurry, so I keep listening.

"What 'The Nose' so vividly demonstrates to us today," says Luzhko, "is that when we blindly believe in someone else's idea of what is right or wrong for us as individuals, sooner or later our refusal to make our own choices could lead to the collapse of the entire political system. An entire country. The world, even."

He looks at the class significantly and says, "Do you understand?"

Of course, they have no idea what he's talking about. This Luzhko is suspicious. I always thought so. All teachers use words you hear on the radio, but he doesn't. I don't know what's wrong with him. I turn and walk away.

The fact is, Vovka is telling on me right now. By the time I get back to Nina Petrovna's class, everyone will know the truth. Right away they'll start treating me like an enemy of the people. And why shouldn't they? My dad is in prison and it is I, not Finkelstein, who damaged Stalin's statue. I am an enemy of the people and I must face the consequences. "The state will bring him up," said the senior lieutenant last night when they took my dad away. I didn't understand it then, but I do now. He was talking about the orphanage. Instead of joining the Pioneers, this is where I'm going. They will feed me, clothe me, and put a roof over my head, but nobody will ever trust me again. From this day on, I will be unreliable and suspicious. Me, who loves Stalin more than any of them! It's hard to believe this is really happening, but it is. I don't have to keep thinking any harder to know what I have to do. I'm going to disappear.

I turn and run back across the main hall, push open the doors to the staircase, and race all the way down. At the bottom of the stairs, I hop over the banister and land right in front of the same senior lieutenant and his two guards.

DISSECTED FROGS, foul chemicals, and something else stomach-turning, all pickled in jars. The biology lab is empty. A good place to hide.

The senior lieutenant recognized me right away and opened his mouth to speak, but I didn't wait to hear. I bolted back up the stairs to this room. Nobody ever comes here since Arnold Moiseevich, a foreign spy pretending to be a biology teacher, was arrested three months ago.

Now, peering through the keyhole, I watch them marching up to the principal's office. I notice that one guard is missing. I bet he's guarding the front door. There's a second exit through the gym; as soon as they are out of sight, I'll sneak in there, and then it's good-bye.

Just then, a nasal voice says behind my back, "For some people, four walls are three too many. One wall's enough for a firing squad."

I turn around slowly. By the window hangs a cloud of tobacco smoke so thick, I can't see who is talking. Behind the smoke, a chair creaks, and the same voice says, "Do you follow me, Zaichik?"

The smoke drifts away, and now I see who's sitting in that chair—*Comrade Stalin's plaster nose*, and it's smoking a pipe!

"Did we arrest your father?" it says. "Yes, we did. Did you report his criminal activities? No, you didn't. Careless, comrade. Complacent. And naive."

I cough and cover my mouth. The biology lab is small and filling up with smoke fast.

"What is your duty and privilege as a Communist youth?" says Stalin's nose. It doesn't wait for my answer. "Renounce your father, an enemy of the people, and join the Pioneers in the march toward Communism. A simple procedure." The nose blows more smoke and rubs its boots together. "Repeat after me. 'I, Sasha Zaichik, renounce my father as an agent of foreign powers and hereby sever all my relations with him. From now on my real father is our beloved Leader and Teacher, Comrade Stalin, and the Young Soviet Pioneers are my family.'"

Carefully, I step back to the door, keeping my eyes on the nose, and pull on the door handle. The door won't budge. It's locked. The nose stares at me, waiting for me to repeat after it.

"What is my father guilty of?" I say.

"We are, at this very moment, in the process of interrogating him. He's about to confess."

"My dad is innocent. There's nothing to confess!"

"Everybody confesses in Lubyanka. We know how to make people talk."

Stalin's nose looks at the pipe and says, "Which

reminds me of an incident. Once, I received a dele-gation of workers from the provinces. When they left, I looked for my pipe but did not see it. I called the chairman of the State Security. 'Nikolai Ivanych, my pipe disappeared after the visit of the workers.' 'Yes, Comrade Stalin, I'll immediately take the proper measures.' Ten minutes later, I pulled out a drawer in my desk and saw my pipe. I dialed the State Security again. 'Nikolai Ivanych, my pipe's been found.' 'What a shame,' he said. 'All of the workers have already confessed.'"

Stalin's nose slaps its knee and laughs, but it's not really a laugh. It's shaking all over and smoke pumps out the nostrils. It's horrible. "Join the Pio-neers, Zaichik, and forget about your father. It's not like you'll ever see him again."

26

"THERE'S NO PLACE for the likes of you in our class," Nina Petrovna says. "Go sit in the back and don't stick your spy nose into anything. Is that clear?"

I'm trying to stop shivering, but the classroom is freezing and I'm soaked through. When Agafia, the cleaning woman, found me in the biology lab, I had passed out. She doused me with icy water to wake me up. Of course I kept quiet about Stalin's nose. I don't want them to think I'm crazy, on top of everything else.

"When you hear the song 'A Bright Future Is

Open to Us,'" says Nina Petrovna, "you begin marching. The drums and the bugles march in first, then the children who will be joining. Remember, class, our great Leader and Teacher is always watching us from the Kremlin. Make him proud. Ready? One, two, three..."

They bugle, drum, and march around Nina Petrovna's desk. From the back row, the classroom looks different. I'm here with other *unreliables* and I can see much better from here. Now I can see the whole room.

"After the song, you will hear a drumroll. This is when our sacred banner will be brought in," says Nina Petrovna, and glances at me. "Who's going to carry the banner? Who truly deserves it? Who loves Stalin most of all?"

She's not looking at me now, but I can tell she's enjoying choosing someone else to carry the banner. Someone other than me.

I look up at our class photograph. Finkelstein's

face is covered in black ink, and Vovka's, too. Mine's next. Any minute, the State Security guards will burst through the door and drag me off to Lubyanka to confess to my crimes. I will never be a Pioneer. Do I still have to live by the rules of the Pioneers?

I get up, walk to where the banner is leaning against the wall, take it, and climb up on Nina Petrovna's desk. I wave the sacred cloth over my head and, marching in place, sing "A Bright Future Is Open to Us" in a loud voice. It feels good.

"Zaichik!" shrieks Nina Petrovna. "Down, Zaichik! Down!"

She tries to grab my foot, but I'm faster. I hop from desk to desk, shouting the song and waving the banner. Nina Petrovna chases after me. Everyone's laughing. Then I miss a desktop and go down, and right away she's on top of me, screeching and wrestling the banner out of my hands.

When the State Security guards stomp in, I'm on my back, head toward the door, so I see their boots upside down. One of the guards is holding Vovka by the collar. "That scum there," Vovka says, pointing in our direction. Then Vovka nods toward Nina Petrovna's desk.

A guard steps over us, clomps to the desk, pulls the drawer out, and dumps it on the floor. Everyone's quiet, watching him. He sorts through the stuff from the drawer with the tip of his boot, then bends down and picks something up.

It's Stalin's plaster nose.

He shoves it into Nina Petrovna's face, which drains to white. "No. No. It's not mine. I couldn't . . . I'm a Communist. . . . It's a mistake."

I look up at Vovka. He knows I'm looking at him, but he doesn't turn his head. I see he's grinning. So, he didn't turn me in after all. He must

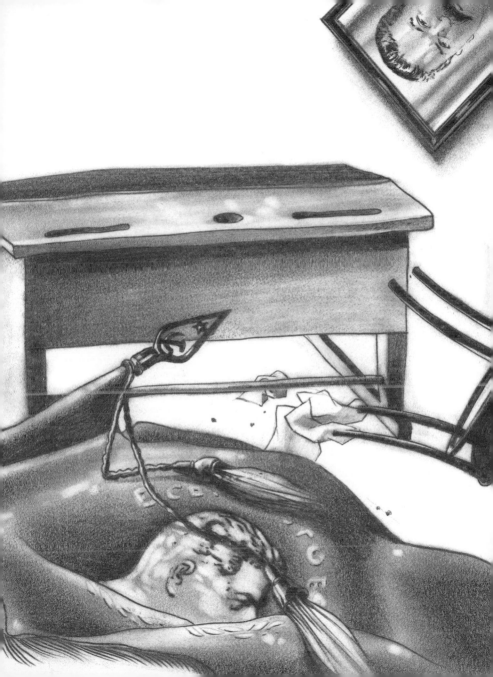

have stayed behind in the classroom and hidden the nose in Nina Petrovna's desk during Sergei Ivanych's speech in the cafeteria.

The guards twist Nina Petrovna's arms and drag her to the door. She screams and kicks and tries to hold on to nearby kids. They duck under her arms, laughing.

I DIDN'T KNOW our principal, Sergei Ivanych, is so short. He's always either behind his desk or behind the podium, delivering speeches. There must be something hidden under his seat to lift him up, because now, as he walks me down the hall, I see that he is no taller than a kid.

"Nina Petrovna didn't break off the nose," I say.

"That woman is no longer my responsibility," he says, and keeps walking.

"Finkelstein didn't break it, either."

"Finkelstein confessed in front of everybody."

"He did it to get into Lubyanka to look for his parents."

"His parents were executed," he says, and shrugs. "Somebody should have told him."

I'm getting the shivers again. My teeth start to chatter. Poor Four-Eyes. His aunt told him his parents had been shot; why didn't he believe her? Now he's gone to prison for nothing.

"No stopping. Let's go, Zaichik," says Sergei Ivanych, and he grabs my arm and pulls me down the stairs to the basement. He's short but strong.

28

SERGEI IVANYCH knocks softly on the storage room door: three quick knocks, a pause, three quick ones again. He listens for a moment, takes a key out of his pocket, unlocks the door, and nudges me in. "Good luck, Zaichik," he says, and shuts the door.

I expect to see Matveich in here, guarding state property, but, in fact, I see nothing, just darkness. I listen to Sergei Ivanych locking the door and walking away and wait for my eyes to adjust to the dark. I grope for the wall and find it clammy to the touch. I feel my way along the wall, boots wading through what feels like shallow water. Soon I bump into

something large and smooth, and I turn to it. I slide my hands over the plaster crevices, and when I find the face, the nose is missing. *So this is where they hauled you, Comrade Stalin, into this dark and moldy place.*

A faint yellow light flickers from the doorway of some room farther in. It gives off enough light for me to make out the shapes of the things around me. At my feet is Vovka's prize watercolor, *Comrade Stalin at the Helm*, the colors running in streaks behind the cracked glass. Next, leaning against the wall and buckling in the water, are dozens of group photographs, the kids' and teachers' faces blackened, scratched, or stabbed out with something sharp. It's creepy.

"Out of sight, out of mind. That's why they put all this stuff down here," says a hoarse voice from the dark. "It helps people forget."

When I turn to the voice, I see the State Security

senior lieutenant sitting on a wooden crate under a dim lightbulb, smiling at me. "Have a seat, Zaichik," he says, and waves at another crate nearby. "Make yourself comfortable." The crate is overflowing with the lists of suspects they made us write. I hesitate and glance at the senior lieutenant, but he nods, so I sit on top of the names.

"Treat yourself," he says, holding a small tin box with hard candies inside. "Take as many as you want." I take one, but he keeps the box open, staring at me, smiling. I take another. "Do you mind if I read something to you?" he says.

I shrug and he takes out a piece of paper and unfolds it carefully. He clears his throat and starts reading. "'It's not possible to be a true Pioneer without training one's character in the Stalinist spirit. I solemnly promise to make myself strong from physical exercise, to forge my Communist character, and always to be vigilant, because our capitalist enemies are never asleep. I will not rest until I am truly useful to my beloved Soviet land and to you personally, dear Comrade Stalin. Thank you for giving me such a wonderful opportunity.'"

It's the letter I wrote yesterday, which my dad was supposed to deliver to Stalin.

"I found it in your dad's briefcase." He leans in close and pats me on the knee. "After all that's happened, do you still want to become a Pioneer?"

"I will not renounce my dad," I say.

"You won't have to, Zaichik. In your case, we're willing to make an exception." Speaking in a secretive voice, he continues: "We're offering you a rare opportunity to pledge assistance to the Soviet State Security. All you have to do is listen in, observe, and report suspicious behavior right here in your own school. Let your deep-felt devotion to Communism be your guide. You'll be our secret agent, like your dad. Comrade Stalin called him 'an iron broom

purging the vermin from our midst.' You bring us enough reports, Zaichik, and you'll get to meet Stalin, too. Imagine that."

"My dad was never a snitch."

"What do you think your dad's job was?" he says, surprised.

He moves his crate so it's touching mine and wraps his arm over my shoulders. This close, I can smell him. Tobacco, sweat, and something else. Gunpowder, I decide.

"Frankly, Zaichik, I used to have great respect for your dad. Two years ago, when he submitted a report on the anti-Communist activity of a certain foreign national, who happened to be his wife—I'm talking about your mother here—he acted as a true Communist, willing to make a personal sacrifice for the good of the common cause."

He's lying. "My mom died in the hospital," I say.

He looks at me strangely and continues: "But

with time, your father's vigilance faltered and he became easy prey for your mother's spy contacts."

"My mother wasn't a spy."

I try to get up, but his arm keeps me seated. "He confessed, Sasha," he says.

"Everybody confesses in Lubyanka," I say, repeating what Stalin's nose said. "You know how to make people talk."

"I understand. It's a lot to take in. But I'm giving you a chance to make the right choice. If you carry the banner today at the Pioneers rally, everybody will be looking at you and thinking, There goes Sasha Zaichik; he's one of us again." He moves his right hand toward me, palm open, waiting for me to shake it. "If you chose not to, I'll be talking to you in the basement of Lubyanka prison. You don't want this to happen, do you, Sasha?"

I look at him. He means it. I shake his hand.

29

THEY ARE DRUMMING and bugling and singing in the darkened hallway. "A Bright Future Is Open to Us." I know every word, but this time I don't sing as I watch the future Pioneers march away, melting into the brilliant lights of the main hall. Alone now, I heave the banner over my shoulder and listen for the drumroll, my cue to follow.

I have waited for this moment all my life. I wanted it so badly. I would imagine myself marching into the main hall, beaming with pride, all eyes upon me. Then I'd see myself standing on a podium beneath the huge face of Stalin, eager for my turn to have the Pioneers scarf tied around my neck. How happy I felt when my dad told me he would tie my scarf. I could see it: He'd step up to me, lay the scarf across my shoulders, tie the knot as the rule says—the right tip extending lower than the left—then would call to me in his strong but kind voice, "Young Pioneer! Ready to fight for the cause of the Communist Party and Comrade Stalin?"

I set the banner down and lean it against the wall. I need my hands to dry my eyes, which are filling with tears. Right then, I hear the drumroll. It throbs and breaks off. It's my turn.

I think of everybody in the main hall listening to the drumroll again and again, eyeing the entrance through which I am to enter, wondering what's holding me up. I see their faces—the kids', the teachers', the janitor Matveich's, the cleaning lady Agafia's, Principal Sergei Ivanych's, and, next to the podium, that of the State Security senior lieutenant who has replaced my dad as guest of honor. My dad, who is in prison. My dad, who said last night, "Tomorrow's a big day." He was right. It was a big day. It changed my life forever.

I take a last look at the banner, turn away, and dash out the back door, down the stairs, and out of the school. I don't want to be a Pioneer.

THIS STREETCAR is like an ice cave. The frost inside the glass makes the windows glow white. I lean in and breathe on the glass. A small circle opens like a peephole in a prison cell's door. I see shiny black automobiles tear through the snow toward a giant yellow building. Somewhere in that building, my dad is in prison.

"Lubyanka Square!" cries the conductor. The streetcar screeches to a stop and the ice-crusted doors begin to part. I squeeze out and hop off and cross the square.

"Step back!" barks the guard, yanking the rifle off his shoulder. I keep going, so he aims the rifle at me. He looks like he'd shoot a kid, so I stop.

"My dad is in prison here," I say. "I need to see him."

Keeping me in his gun sights, the guard nods toward the edge of the building.

"Around the corner?" I say.

He nods again.

What I see when I round the corner, I don't expect. It's a line of people who must be waiting to see prisoners. The line runs along the building and across the street and down the next street and up the next one, and by the time I reach the end, I pass thousands of people waiting. I get in line.

After a while, a woman in front of me turns around. "You must be cold," she says. "Where are your warm things?"

I shrug. She stares at me for a moment, then digs into her bag and pulls out a woolen scarf. "I made this for my son," she says. "Wrap it around. I'll take it back when we get to the door."

I wrap the scarf around my neck and ears and she helps me with it. Her scarf is warm.

"Both of your parents in there?"

I shake my head. "My dad."

"Where's your mom?"

"She died. In the hospital," I quickly explain.

She looks at me sadly, and I say, "My dad didn't take me to the funeral. I still have to ask him why."

"Funerals are sad," she says.

That's when I know why he didn't take me. He didn't want me to be sad.

"What about relatives? Uncles? Aunts?"

I think about Aunt Larisa and say, "No. Don't have any."

"Where do you live?"

I shrug again.

"Homeless," she says, and shakes her head. "Good thing you won't need a bed for the next three nights. That's how long it'll take you to see your dad."

I don't mind. I have nowhere else to go. She doesn't even ask if I'm hungry, just takes out something wrapped in a cloth and hands it to me. I unwrap it—a baked potato, still hot. She stares at me while I eat it.

"What's your name?" she says.

"Sasha Zaichik."

"I tell you what, Sasha Zaichik. Now that my son's cot is empty, you're welcome to it if you want."

I look up at her and see that she's smiling. Her smile is kind and natural.

I should ask my dad, I think, but instead I say, "Sounds good. Thank you."

She nods, then looks up at the low sky. It's snowing again.

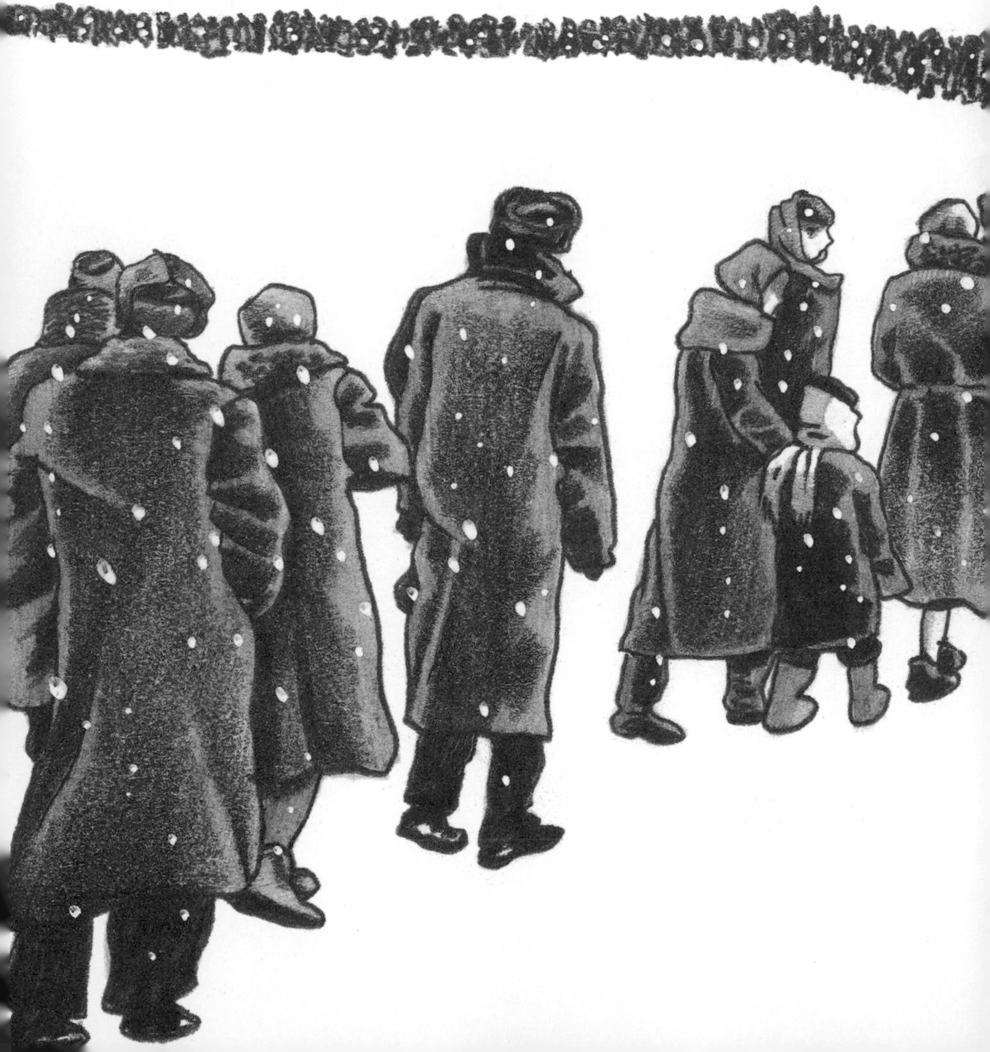

"What a mess we got ourselves into, huh, Zaichik? Think we can sort it out one day?"

I don't know.

"We will," she says. "But for now, we have a lot of waiting to do. So let's wait, Zaichik."

And we do.

THE END

AUTHOR'S NOTE

An official from the Committee of State Security once called me in for an "informal" chat. A typical Soviet secret policeman, he locked the door of his office, put the key in his pocket, and invited me to discuss the political views of my coworkers. His goal was to recruit me as an informer. I had no idea what would happen to my family or to me were I to refuse, but I suspected bad things. The State Security terrified everyone, and I was afraid. But I could never become a snitch, either. For two straight hours, I played dumb, evading questions and pretending I didn't understand him. He got bored, unlocked the door, and finally let me go. I felt insulted and humiliated, but I was not harmed. Had that happened some years earlier, when the ruthless dictator

Joseph Stalin ruled Russia, I would not have gotten out of that office alive.

During his reign, from 1923 to 1953, Joseph Stalin ensured his absolute power by waging war against the Russian people. Stalin's State Security executed, imprisoned, or exiled over twenty million people. Not a single person, be it a government official, war hero, worker, teacher, or homemaker, could be certain he or she would not be arrested.

To arrest so many innocent people, crimes had to be invented. Stalin's propaganda machine deceived ordinary people into believing that countless spies and terrorists threatened their security. Tormented by fear, Soviet citizens clung to Stalin for guidance and protection, and soon his popularity reached cult status. "The father of all Soviet children" smiled and waved at his supporters during parades and celebrations, while at night, in his Kremlin office, he was signing orders for innocent people to be shot without trial.

Paradoxically, when I was growing up in the 1960s Soviet Union, few people of my generation were aware of what had transpired under Stalin. During his lifetime, the crimes had been carried out in absolute secrecy. After his death, the secrecy continued: All evidence was classi-fied or destroyed. Older generations, either still terrified or responsible for the crimes, kept silent.

But Stalin could not simply disappear; his legacy endured in the Russian people. They had lived in fear for so long that fear had become an integral part of their very beings. Unchecked, fear was passed on from generation to generation. It has been passed on to me, as well.

This book is my attempt to expose and confront that fear. Like my main character, I wanted to be a Young Pioneer. My family shared a communal apartment. My father was a devoted Communist. And like my main character, I, too, had to make a choice. My choice was about whether to leave the country of my birth.

I set this story in the past, but the main issue in it transcends time and place. To this day, there are places in the world where innocent people face persecution and death for making a choice about what they believe to be right.

—*Eugene Yelchin*
Los Angeles, California

SASHA'S MOSCOW

In order to warn Comrade Stalin about the arrest of his father, Sasha walks to the Kremlin. Sasha is sure that even in the middle of the night, Comrade Stalin would not be asleep. The great leader works long hours; the windows in his office are always lit. What Sasha doesn't know is that Stalin doesn't spend nights in the Kremlin. He has several homes outside of Moscow. The homes' locations are a state secret. But even when Stalin is not in the Kremlin, the light in his office is kept on.

SASHA'S APARTMENT

This is a map of Sasha's communal apartment, or *komunalka*, for short: 1) The front entrance leads into 2) a common kitchen with 3) a stove with twelve rings, 4) a toilet, and 5) a sink with a cold-water tap. 6) A corridor runs the length of the apartment with single rooms on either side. 7) A cubbyhole is occupied by Marfa Ivanovna, an elderly peasant woman. Another tenant without a room is Semenov, a Civil War invalid who sleeps behind a curtain in the corridor. 8) through 19) are single-family rooms. 48 people in all, from factory workers to opera singers are living under one roof. Sasha's room is number 12, the biggest and most envied room in the apartment.

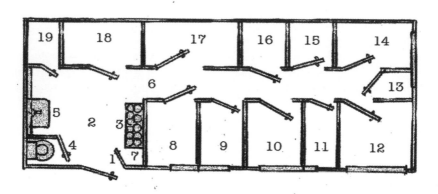

During a celebration in the Kremlin, Comrade Stalin personally pins the Order of the Red Banner on Sasha's dad's chest, calling him "an iron broom purging the vermin from our midst." A photographer snaps a picture of this historic moment. Afterward, Comrade Stalin likes the photograph so much, he orders to turn it into a poster celebrating great achievements of the State Security. In the poster, Sasha's dad's likeness is altered in order, Sasha believes, to keep his dad's identity secret.

THE SECRET POLICEMAN'S BADGE

This is the secret police officer's badge that Sasha's dad wears on his uniform. Sasha likes to imagine his fearless dad fighting the enemies of the people with the sword rendered on this badge.

SASHA'S MOM

From the questionnaire Sasha's mom filled out upon her arrival, the Soviet officials learned that she held a job for the Ford Motor Company in Detroit, Michigan. Sasha's mom was dispatched to a city called Gorky, where Ford built an enormous auto factory. Many Americans were employed at the factory, assembling Ford cars and trucks for Soviet roads. Sasha's mom was assigned to work in the machine shop, sorting out English labels for the Russian mechanics.

YOUNG SOVIET PIONEERS

Comrade Stalin takes good care of the Young Pioneers.
Thousands of Pioneer palaces are built across the USSR.
When the schools are out for the summer, the Young Pioneers spend their vacations in Pioneer
camps. The camps are free of charge.
There, the Young Pioneers make them-
selves strong with physical exercise.
They learn to be vigilant because their
capitalist enemies never sleep.

160

☆ ☆ INFORMERS ☆ ☆

To unmask the enemies of the people, the secret police use an army of informers. They listen in on conversations and report suspicious behavior. Most informers are paid, while others receive favors from the secret police. Informing becomes a profitable activity. Sasha's dad says that nearly one in five Soviet citizens is an informer.

☆ ☆ LUBYANKA ☆ ☆

Sasha's dad's office is on the third floor of this yellow-brick building on Lubyanka Square in Moscow, the headquarters of the secret police. Sasha is not allowed to visit his dad in his office, but later, this is where Sasha comes to visit his dad in prison.

QUESTIONS FOR THE AUTHOR
  # EUGENE YELCHIN

WHAT IS YOUR FAVORITE CHILDHOOD MEMORY?

The communal apartment where Sasha Zaichik lives with his father is similar to the one I grew up in. In addition to my family, several other families had to share one kitchen, one toilet, and one sink with a cold-water tap. My father and mother, my grandmother, and my brother and I were crowded into one small room. At night when the sofas, cots, and folding chairs were converted into beds, the only room left for my small cot was under our round dinner table. I didn't mind sleeping under the table; the space was cozy and gave me much-needed privacy. I still remember pencil marks that a carpenter who built the table had left on the bottom of the tabletop. One night, I snuck in a pencil and began adding my own scribbles to his. Soon, the bottom of the tabletop was covered with my drawings that no one knew about. For the first time, I felt the power of creating a world that was all my own. This is my favorite childhood memory because I believe that secretly drawing on the underside of that table triggered my future life as an artist.

AS A YOUNG PERSON, WHO DID YOU LOOK UP TO MOST?

Like most young boys, I was taken with my father. He seemed solid and strong to me then, but looking back now, I'm amazed what a paradoxical man he actually was. My father was a tough, competitive soccer player who at the same time was fond of Russian poetry and loved to recite it to his teammates! But his main contradiction was this: He understood the oppressive reality of living under communism, yet he was a devoted Communist. That paradox was lost on me then. As a kid, I didn't know our reality was oppressive; I didn't know of any other. Having a Communist father, I took the Communist ideals for granted. Only later as a teenager did I begin questioning my father's beliefs, which consequently created a rift between us. The disillusionment with my father's Communist ideals ran parallel to my own maturity. Year after year, I was shedding my father's sway over me while struggling not to lose my love for him.

WHAT WAS YOUR FAVORITE BOOK WHEN YOU WERE A KID?

When I was a kid, good books in Russia were hard to come by. The government controlled the publishing industry. Millions of copies of mediocre propagandistic works were published, while outstanding authors were suppressed. Even Russian classics were available by subscription only. In order to subscribe, one had to spend untold hours waiting in line, often at night under a heavy snowfall. My father was able to collect a unique library through such subscriptions. In all likelihood, it took my father the same amount of time to read a book as it took him to stand in line in order to get to it. But back then, I didn't care much about Russian classics. All I wanted was to get my hands on one very special set of illustrated books my father didn't have, called *The Adventure and Science Fiction Library*. Luckily, friends of my parents were able to secure a subscription, and every Sunday while visiting with them, I'd lose track of time poring over those precious volumes. Years later, the family who owned the books was able to immigrate to the United States. They settled in Minneapolis and I flew in to see them. Amazingly, they brought *The Adventure and Science Fiction Library* along. My hands shook when I pulled these books off the shelf. Over forty years had passed since I'd last opened them. In that distant past, I must have read these books very closely and looked at the pictures even closer because I remembered every single line in the drawings of cowboys, knights, and pirates that I'd loved so much as a child.

WHICH OF YOUR CHARACTERS IS MOST LIKE YOU?

Definitely not the teacher Nina Petrovna. She is a combined portrait of many such teachers I had in grade school. I still get shivers thinking of them. But Sasha Zaichik's character is close to mine. Not because I also wanted to become a Young Soviet Pioneer, or because my own family shared an overcrowded communal apartment, or because my father was a Communist. Sasha and I are similar in the way we react to the world around us. We want to believe that the real world is a better place than it so often is. We are always surprised when we come face to face with brutality, unfairness, or lies. And someplace deep inside both of us, we have a moral line we would never cross, no matter what our circumstances are.

WHAT KIND OF RESEARCH DID YOU DO FOR THIS NOVEL?

Much of the novel is autobiographical, but because the story takes place before I was born, some historical research was necessary. I began reading books about Stalinism, personal diaries preserved from that period, and some archival materials. I must admit, it took a considerable amount of emotional and psychological strength to keep at it. The world that opened up before me was oppressive and dark. All of my schooling in

Russia—elementary, middle, high school, and college—happened under Communist rule. Any information about the crimes of Stalinism had been repressed. Any attempt to gather or disseminate such information was severely punished. Now, I was living in America, a citizen, a father myself, but for the first time in my life, I was discovering the full extent of the events I had been only vaguely aware of. As a result, my research for the novel grew into something much bigger; it affected me personally. I realized it was my duty to tell the truth. My book became necessary.

WHAT DO YOU CONSIDER TO BE YOUR GREATEST ACCOMPLISHMENT?

What I value most is the ability to make a personal choice in spite of circumstances. Often, it seems impossible to make such a choice because of peer or family pressure or fear of repercussions. My greatest accomplishment may not seem significant to others. It is not the awards, or the published books, or my art exhibitions. My greatest accomplishment was to dare leaving behind the country of my birth. Compared to so many others, my life in Russia was good at the time. I had a successful artistic career, respect, and food on my table. I was and still am proud to be a part of such a rich Russian culture. Yet, deep inside, I knew that to remain a citizen of the Soviet Union would implicate me in the crimes of my government. I did everything I could to leave Russia. But that is another story.

FIND OUT MORE ABOUT

BREAKING STALIN'S NOSE

☆ **EXPLORE SASHA'S MOSCOW** ☆

breakingstalinsnose.com

☆ **WATCH THE BOOK TRAILER** ☆

http://www.youtube.com/watch?v=nV6gghKDuWY

☆ **DOWNLOAD THE DISCUSSION GUIDE** ☆

us.macmillan.com/breakingstalinsnose/EugeneYelchin